INGRI & EDGAR ON LIA
WILTON CONN.

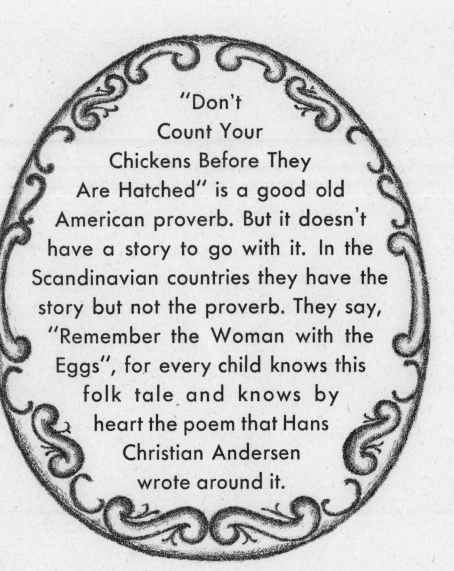

"Don't
Count Your
Chickens Before They
Are Hatched" is a good old
American proverb. But it doesn't
have a story to go with it. In the
Scandinavian countries they have the
story but not the proverb. They say,
"Remember the Woman with the
Eggs", for every child knows this
folk tale and knows by
heart the poem that Hans
Christian Andersen
wrote around it.

DON'T COUNT YOUR CHICKS

INGRI & EDGAR PARIN D'AULAIRE

THE JUNIOR LITERARY GUILD AND
DOUBLEDAY, DORAN & CO., INC. GARDEN CITY, N.Y. 1943

The Drawings for this book were lithographed directly on stone by the artists
and the book was printed in four colors by George C. Miller, New York,
in the United States of America.

D239d

"Cock-a-doodle-do! The moon is still in the sky but soon the sun will open its eye, now I have opened mine," crowed the cock.

"Gack, gack," replied the hen and laid an egg.

"Gack, gack, gack, I have laid an egg," sang the hen. "Cock-a-doodle-do," crowed the cock for he was as proud as if he had laid the egg himself.

That woke up the old woman who owned the hen.

And wasn't she pleased!

"Oh dear, oh dear, what a hen I have," the old woman spoke to herself. "Other hens lay once in a while, but mine never misses a day."

And then she started to wonder and figure how many eggs she might have on her egg shelf.

Three dozen she counted and all of them fresh. "I'll take them to town and sell them," she thought.

So she put out the cat, tied up the dog and hid her door key under the doorstep.

And off she set to walk to town with her basket full of eggs.

Uphill and downhill walked the old woman. She walked as fast

as she could, but the way was long and she was alone.

So after a while she started to think to make the time run faster.

"How much will I get for my eggs?" she thought.

She counted eggs and dollars and cents and she looked neither to the right nor to the left until she had finished counting.

She counted so many eggs and dollars and cents that she beamed at the thought of all she would get for her eggs.

Now, let me see, "she wondered and figured, "what shall I do when I get all that money? I'll buy two hens, "she spoke to herself." Then, with my good old hen I'll have three.

My three hens will lay three eggs a day, and soon I will be on my way to market again with three times as many eggs as today.

And then I will buy three more hens. Three I have. So that will make six.

All six will lay an egg a day. Half of the eggs I'll sell.

As for the rest my hens will hatch them. Yes, that will be best.

And soon I'll have a henhouse full. Some hens will lay and some

will hatch. Oh, dear me, will I be rich!

I'll buy two geese and a little lamb.

The lamb I'll shear and the geese I'll pluck.

So with eggs and chickens and down and wool it won't be long before I have my penny pig bursting full.

Then I'll buy a real pig. No, wait, I think I had better buy two. One pig gets lonesome, while two get fat. I'll also buy a milking cow.

Eggs and chickens, geese and sheep, down and wool, pigs and cow, hams and bacon, milk and cream! Hurrah! Then I'll hire a maid and a man. I'll make them run from morning till night and carry out my wishes. They won't dare to answer me back, for I am their mistress.

Then, one day a suitor will come. I will marry him for sure,

for he has a farm still bigger than mine.

And now I'm a lady.

I shall be so fine, and so proud I can turn up my nose at everything.

Yes, I'll know how to turn up my nose." But as she said it

she did it. Crash! There lay the eggs on the ground.

"Oh my, oh my," cried the old woman. "Why did my riches make me so proud? There I lost suitor and servants and milk and cream and hams and bacon and pigs and cow, and down and wool and geese and sheep and chickens and even the eggs in my basket, oh dear.

But maybe it isn't so bad after all," thought the old woman as she came home again. "I have my good little house to live in, my dog and cat to keep me from being alone, my cock to wake me up in the morning, and my hen who is so good she lays an egg a day. How lucky I am to have so good a hen."